Twinkle, Twinkle, Little Star

Twinkle, Twinkle, Little Star

As told and illustrated by

Iza Trapani

SCHOLASTIC INC.
New York   Toronto   London   Auckland   Sydney

A special thanks to Anne Marie for opening the door,
and to Lou for letting me in.

ISBN 0-590-97551-X

12 11 10 9 8 7 6 5 4 3 2 1   6 7 8 9/9 0 1/0

Printed in the U.S.A.   08

First Scholastic printing, September 1996

For Aimee, Kyle, Rebecca, and Sophie—
some of the brightest little stars I know.

Twinkle, twinkle, little star,
How I wonder what you are!
Up above the world so high,
Like a diamond in the sky.
Twinkle, twinkle, little star,
How I wonder what you are

Twinkle, twinkle, star so bright,
Winking at me in the night.
How I wish that I could fly,
And visit you up in the sky.
I wish I may, I wish I might,
Have the wish I wish tonight.

Little child, your wish came true,
Here I am right next to you.
I'll take you on a magic ride,
So come with me—I'll be your guide.
There's so much that you'll see and do,
On this adventure made for you.

Out your window, through the sky,
Up above the world we'll fly,
Higher than a bird would go,
To places only rockets know.
Beyond the planes that soar up high,
Is where we'll travel, you and I.

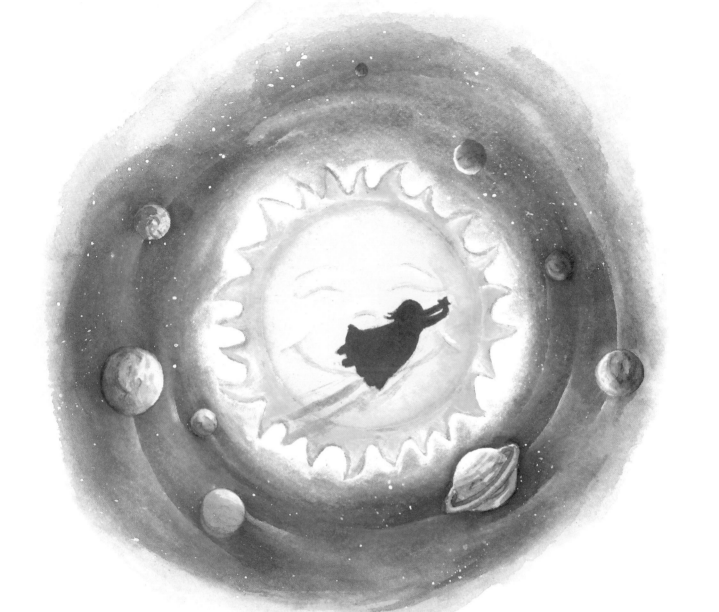

Look around you, little one,
There's the moon and there's the sun.
See the planets—count them all,
Some are big and some are small.
Can you name them one by one,
As they orbit 'round the sun?

Your planet Earth is such a sight,
I look at her with great delight.
When half the earth is in the sun,
The other half I glow upon.
For it's my job to twinkle bright,
On everyone who needs my light.

I shine on ships lost out at sea,
They know they can depend on me.
For even on the darkest nights,
I guide them to their harbor lights.
And lonely travelers wandering free,
Will find their way back home with me.

Everywhere I look below,
I shed my light and cast a glow.
Over cities, over farms,
On babies held in loving arms.
How I love to watch them grow,
As I shine on Earth below.

Little child, look down with me,
And tell me, tell me, what you see.
I see puppies in their bed,
A pony resting in his shed.
Little birds high in a tree,
And sleepy children just like me.

Yes, it's late—we can't pretend,
Our magic journey has to end.
I'll take you home, back to your bed,
You'll see me twinkling overhead.
But don't be sad—I do intend,
To shine on you each night, my friend.

Twinkle bright, my little star,
Watch me safely from afar.
Thank you for this magic night,
And the comfort of your light.
Twinkle, twinkle, little star,
What a special star you are!

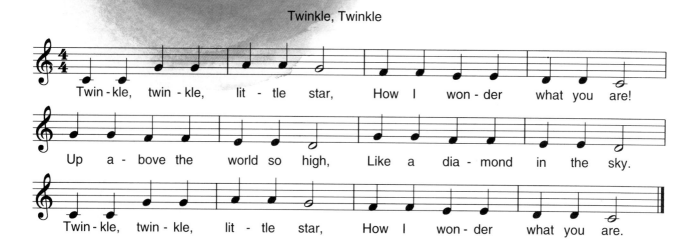

Twinkle, Twinkle

Twin - kle, twin - kle, lit - tle star, How I won - der what you are!

Up a - bove the world so high, Like a dia - mond in the sky.

Twin - kle, twin - kle, lit - tle star, How I won - der what you are.

2. Twinkle, twinkle, star so bright,
Winking at me in the night.
How I wish that I could fly,
And visit you up in the sky.
I wish I may, I wish I might,
Have the wish I wish tonight.

3. Little child, your wish came true,
Here I am right next to you.
I'll take you on a magic ride,
So come with me—I'll be your guide.
There's so much you'll see and do,
On this adventure made for you.

4. Out your window, through the sky,
Up above the world we'll fly.
Higher than a bird would go,
To places only rockets know.
Beyond the planes that soar up high,
Is where we'll travel, you and I.

5. Look around you, little one,
There's the moon and there's the sun.
See the planets—count them all,
Some are big and some are small.
Can you name them one by one,
As they orbit 'round the sun?

6. Your planet Earth is such a sight,
I look at her with great delight.
When half the earth is in the sun,
The other half I glow upon.
For it's my job to twinkle bright,
On everyone who needs my light.

7. I shine on ships lost out at sea,
They know they can depend on me.
For even on the darkest nights,
I guide them to their harbor lights.
And lonely travelers wandering free,
Will find their way back home with me.

8. Everywhere I look below,
I shed my light and cast a glow.
Over cities, over farms,
On babies held in loving arms.
How I love to watch them grow,
As I shine on Earth below.

9. Little child, look down with me,
And tell me, tell me, what you see.
I see puppies in their bed,
A pony resting in his shed.
Little birds high in a tree,
And sleepy children just like me.

10. Yes, it's late—we can't pretend,
Our magic journey has to end.
I'll take you home, back to your bed,
You'll see me twinkling overhead.
But don't be sad—I do intend,
To shine on you each night, my friend.

11. Twinkle bright, my little star,
Watch me safely from afar.
Thank you for this magic night,
And the comfort of your light.
Twinkle, twinkle, little star,
What a special star you are!